Spot Bakes a Cake

Eric Hill

PUFFIN BOOKS

It's your dad's
on Friday

We have to go

shopping.

Can you

find the chocolate, Spot?

Now we can

make the cake.

The cake is in the

oven. Help me
clean up, Spot!

Can I decorate

yet,

the cake
Mom?

Go easy

on the icing, Spot!

nice surprise for
dad, Spot.

Happy Birthday Dad!

birthday, Dad!

you make the cake, Spot? It's delicious!

Thanks, Dad. Mom helped a little.

FREDERICK WARNE
Published by the Penguin Group
Penguin Group (USA) LLC, 375 Hudson Street, New York, New York 10014, USA

USA | Canada | UK | Ireland | Australia | New Zealand | India | South Africa | China

penguin.com
A Penguin Random House Company

First published by Frederick Warne & Co., 1994. Published by Puffin Books in 1996. This edition published by Frederick Warne & Co., 2015. Copyright © 1994 by Eric Hill. All rights reserved. The moral right of the author has been asserted. Manufactured in China.

ISBN 978–0–14–240329–7   013